For Gemk,

Whose endless supply of ideas and honest critique made this possible.

感謝 Gemk

源源不絕的靈感及誠懇的建議讓這一切成真。

Hank the Hero

英雄漢克

Coleen Reddy 著

安 宏 繪

薛慧儀 譯

三民書局

Hank wants to be a hero.

He has a book called *How To Be A Hero*.

Hank will read the book. Then he will be a hero.

漢克想要當一個英雄。
他有一本叫做「如何成為英雄」的書。
漢克希望讀了這本書之後，可以變成一個英雄。

Hank reads:

"No. 1: A hero must have a costume."

Hank does not have a costume.

What can he do?

書上說：「英雄守則第一條：每位英雄一定要有一套英雄裝。」
可是漢克沒有英雄裝啊！
他該怎麼辦呢？

5

He opens his closet and looks at his clothes.

He puts on his pajamas. They are old and have lots of holes.

He does not have gloves so he uses his green socks as gloves.

他打開衣櫥，看了看裡面的衣服。

他找了件舊睡衣穿上，上頭還有好幾個破洞呢！

他還缺雙手套，所以就用一雙綠襪子來充當。

He puts his red underpants on his head because he does not have a hood.
He looks at himself in the mirror.
"I look so handsome!" he thinks. "Now I have a costume."

接下來，他需要一頂頭罩，好讓別人看不見他的臉。

但是他也沒有頭罩，於是就用紅內褲套在頭上來充當。

他站在鏡子前，看著自己的模樣。

「我看起來真是帥呆了！」他心想。「現在我有一套英雄裝了！」

Hank reads the book.
"No. 2: A hero must help a girl."
His sister, Jane, is a girl
but she does not need help.

漢克再繼續往下看那本書。
「第二條：英雄一定要解救女生。」
他的妹妹珍就是一個女生，
但是她現在並不需要人家去救她。

Hank gets an idea.

He sneaks into Jane's room when she is not there.

He picks up her favorite doll and breaks its arm off.

Then he runs back to his room and waits.

於是漢克想到一個點子。
他趁珍不在的時候，偷偷溜進她的房間，
拿起她最心愛的娃娃，把娃娃的手臂折斷。
然後他趕緊跑回自己房裡，等著珍的呼救。

13

A few minutes later, Jane screams, "Help! Help!"

Hank runs to her room.

Jane is crying because her doll's arm is broken.

But when she sees Hank in his costume, she starts laughing.

過了幾分鐘，果然聽到珍開始尖叫：「救命哪！救命哪！」
漢克馬上跑到她房間。
珍哭得好傷心喔！因為她的娃娃手臂斷了。
但她一看到穿著英雄裝的漢克，就笑了出來。

Hank gets angry.

"What's wrong?" he asks.

"You look so funny," says his sister, laughing.

漢克生氣了。
「有什麼不對勁嗎？」他問。
「你看起來好好笑喔！」他妹妹邊說邊笑。

"No, I mean, why were you crying for help?" asks Hank.

"My doll's arm is broken," says his sister.

"I will help you because I am a *hero*," says Hank.

He uses some glue and fixes Jane's doll.

"Thank you," says Jane.

「不是啦，我是問你為什麼大叫救命啊？」漢克問。

「我的娃娃手臂斷了。」他妹妹說。

「我來幫你，因為我是英雄。」漢克說。

他用了點膠水將手臂黏回去，把珍的娃娃修好了。

「謝謝你！」珍說。

Hank reads his book.

"No. 3: A hero must kill a monster."

Hank is not sure what a monster is.

He asks his mother.

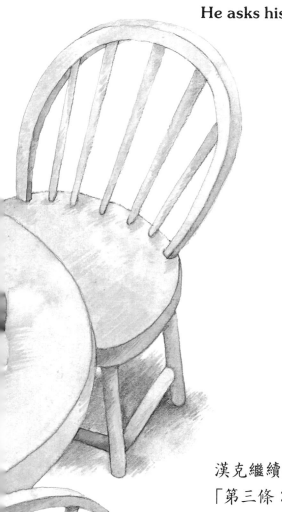

漢克繼續讀那本書。

「第三條：英雄一定要殺掉一隻怪物。」

漢克不太清楚什麼是怪物，就跑去問媽媽。

"Mom, what is a monster?" asks Hank.
"It is something big and bad. It kills humans,"
says his mother.
"Where can I find a monster?" asks Hank.

22

「媽媽，什麼是怪物啊？」漢克問。
「就是一種很大又很壞的東西，
還會殺害人類唷！」媽媽說。
「到哪兒才能找到怪物呢？」漢克問。

"There are no monsters here," says his mother.
"But I need to kill a monster," says Hank.
A housefly is flying over his mother's tea.

「這裡沒有什麼怪物呀!」媽媽說。
「但是我得殺掉一隻怪物才行呀!」漢克說。
這時,有隻蒼蠅繞著媽媽的茶飛來飛去。

His mother does not like the housefly.

"You can kill that housefly for me," says his mother.

"But it is not a monster," says Hank.

媽媽不喜歡蒼蠅。

「你可以幫我打死那隻蒼蠅啊！」媽媽說。

「可是牠又不是怪物。」漢克說。

"Yes," says his mother. "It's a little monster, but it's still a monster."
Hank runs after the fly. He kills the fly with his hand.
"Yes!" he thinks. "Now I am a hero."

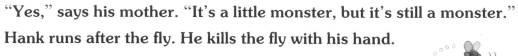

「牠是啊！」媽媽說。「牠雖然長得小，但仍然是一隻怪物喔！」
於是漢克便追著這隻蒼蠅跑，最後用手把牠打死了。
「好棒喔！」漢克心想。「現在我是個英雄了！」

Hank reads his book.
There is one last thing he must do.
"No. 4: Heroes can only eat HAGGIS."
Hank does not know what haggis is.
Maybe it is candy or ice cream.
He asks his father.

漢克繼續讀那本書，現在只剩下最後一件事要做了。
「第四條：英雄只能吃一種叫做『哈吉士』的食物。」
漢克不知道什麼是「哈吉士」。
可能是一種糖果或是冰淇淋吧！
於是他跑去問爸爸。

31

"Dad, what is haggis?"

"Haggis is the heart, liver and lungs of a sheep," says his father.

"People in Scotland like to eat it."

"WHAT!?" yells Hank.

「爸爸，什麼是『哈吉士』呀？」
「『哈吉士』就是羊的心臟和肝肺，
蘇格蘭人很喜歡吃呢！」爸爸說。
「什麼!?」漢克叫了出來。

He runs back to his room and takes off his costume.
He throws the hero book out the window.
"Yuck, I don't want to eat haggis. Who wants to be a stupid hero anyway?"
says Hank as he takes a bite of his favorite chocolate.

他跑回房裡脫掉英雄裝，
還把那本教人如何當英雄的書丟出窗外。
「好噁心喔！我才不要吃『哈吉士』呢！誰要當這種笨英雄啊？」
漢克一面說，一面咬了一口他最喜歡的巧克力。

指頭娃娃

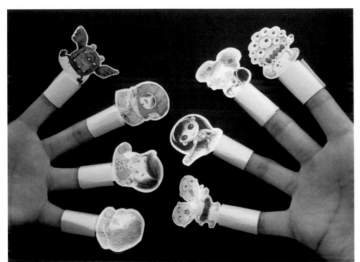

🦋工具與材料

1. 剪刀
2. 膠水或膠帶或雙面膠
3. 西卡紙

步 驟

1. 用西卡紙,依照自己手指頭的大小,做成圓筒。
2. 將右頁附圖剪下,貼在做好的圓筒上。

做好了之後,就可以和兄弟姊妹或朋友
一起玩角色扮演的遊戲囉!

生字表

波波唸翻天系列

你知道可愛的小兔子也會 "碎碎唸" 嗎？
波波就是這樣。
他將要告訴我們什麼有趣的故事呢？

波波的復活節／波波的西部冒險記／波波上課記／我愛你，波波
波波的下雪天／波波郊遊去／波波打球記／聖誕快樂，波波／波波的萬聖夜

共 9 本，每本均附 CD

國家圖書館出版品預行編目資料

Hank the Hero:英雄漢克 / Coleen Reddy著; 安宏
繪; 薛慧儀譯.－－初版一刷.－－臺北市; 三民,
2003
　　面;　　公分－－(愛閱雙語叢書.二十六個妙朋
友系列) 中英對照
ISBN 957－14－3771－9　(精裝)

1.英國語言－讀本

523.38　　　　　　　　　　　　92008837

© Hank the Hero
——英雄漢克

著作人　Coleen Reddy
繪　圖　安　宏
譯　者　薛慧儀
發行人　劉振強
著作財
產權人　三民書局股份有限公司
　　　　臺北市復興北路386號
發行所　三民書局股份有限公司
　　　　地址／臺北市復興北路386號
　　　　電話／(02)25006600
　　　　郵撥／0009998－5
印刷所　三民書局股份有限公司
門市部　復北店／臺北市復興北路386號
　　　　重南店／臺北市重慶南路一段61號
初版一刷　2003年7月
　編　號　S 85641－1
　定　價　新臺幣壹佰捌拾元整
行政院新聞局登記證局版臺業字第○二○○號

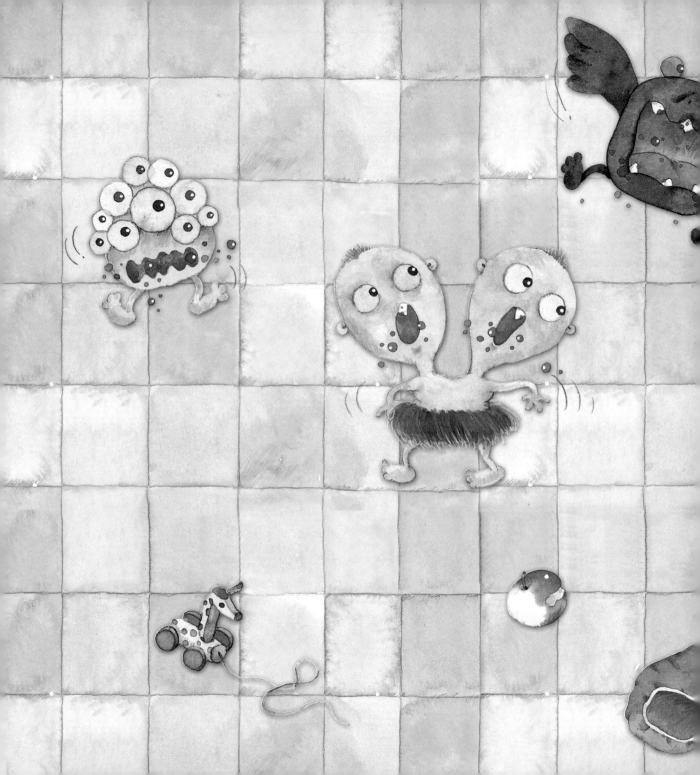